Somewhere In Between

... A children's poetry book for adults

Copyright © 2021 Matthew Eastman

All rights reserved. No part of this book may be reproduced or used in any manner without the prior written permission of the copyright owner, except for the use of brief quotations in a book review.

To request permissions, contact the publisher at lifeandmatt@gmail.com

www.lifeandmatt.com

To everyone who has inspired wonder and whimsy in my life ...

Thank you!

Opening Note from the Poet

I wrote this book for all of us childlike adults
Who are equally excited to grow up
... And not to grow up

My hope is that these words
Will open up the hearts and minds
Of both the young and old
In age and in spirit

Much like the world around us
The community of characters in this book
Tell stories to one another
And share the truths
That exist in the tension
Between the simplicity of curiosity
And the complexity of "reality"

This book is for everyone like me ...

Somewhere in between

Good Poem

We say good morning
We say good night
We say good afternoon
We say good evening
We say good riddance
We say good heavens too
We say good luck
We say good day
We even say good showing
We say good job
We say good deal
We even say good going
Good shape
Good grief
Good sport
Good call

And don't forget good bye!

So why do people giggle
When I say to them good hi?

Somewhere Outside the Mold

The thing I love 'bout poetry

Is there's no such thing as mistakes

I can put a period

Here.

If I want to

Or I can

Space   My   Words   Out

For goodness' sake!

If I want a plus sign +

Or an asterisk *

I can do that!

I can even skip a word and just put in an @

See how I just hopped a line

And made a gap instead

I call it creativity!!

Who says that poems even have to rhyme or flow seamlessly?

You're allowed to write your life

In your very OWN way.

You're even allowed to say … whatever you'd like to say

Don't let them push you 'round
and certainly don't get pulled
Because life is best lived

Somewhere

Outside

The

Mold.

Box of NoThings

Whenever I find new necessary things

I put them in my box

I've got four types of magic tricks and thirty collectible chopsticks

And six pairs of special unworn socks

I've got fifty-two bottle caps and three unused guitar straps

And five crystalline rocks

Eight limited edition balloons, twelve polished silver spoons

And three different decorative clocks

Two alligator skin jackets, ten trading card packets, four signed tennis rackets

And even three Vincent van Gogh smocks

I keep all my prized possessions

Right inside my box

One day on my search for significant stuff

I found a little boy

But unlike me

His box was bare

A vast voluminous void

Never had I ever seen

Such a sad pathetic location

He claimed his box was full to the brim

With "pure imagination"?!

Growing Down

When I woke up this morning I was one foot more small
Twelve inches more low and a ruler less tall
I arose from my bed and walked down the hall
Picked up some chalk and marked on the wall

When I stepped back I was struck by the sight
The marks on the wall reflected my height

As soon as I saw it ... it was suddenly clear!
My direction of growth ... it changes each year!

It's okay to grow down or above between or through
Into or out of ... it's really up to you!

But just growing up? You'll get lost in the sky!
There's a place in the clouds where tall gets too high

When you wake in the morning I hope you won't fret
Your height will keep changing ... just don't grow up yet!

Balloons

I tied balloons around my wrist
Every single day

Hoping that a time would come
When I could fly away

Now I'm stuck here in the sky
I float and drift and roam

I just wish I'd brought a pin
So I could get back home

Home Sick

When I used to feel queasy
Life was real easy

Mom would bring me soup

I'd lie in my bed
While she got my meds

Home sick was pretty darn good

Now when I'm ill
No one brings me pills

And there's no soup in my lap

I'm homesick
For home sick

And I miss those days

Please just bring me back

Dear Professor

I wrote *He and I*
And he wrote *He and me*

I spelled out *goodbye*
And he wrote *howdy-dee*

I used *quantify*
And all he wrote was *see*

I dotted all my *i's*
He didn't cross his *t's*

Dear professor ... *sigh*
Did you forget your answer key?

You scored his paper A
But you scored my paper D!

The City

I'm in a rush to go nowhere
And I'm worried I'll be late
I'm sick of being somewhere
And I just can't stand to wait

What's with these people everywhere?
Do they not have no one to see?
What's the point in being anywhere?
Do they not have nowhere to be?

Why be somewhere doing something with someone?
When you can be nowhere doing nothing every day?
Why be anything anywhere with anyone?
When you can rush everyone and everything away?

Hair

You seem to think that you're all-knowin'
But did you know that hair keeps growin'?

Even when it's gray and slowin'
On windy days you'll see it blowin'

And even if it's barely showin'
Those final hairs will keep on flowin'

As long as life just keeps on goin'
Remember hair just keeps on growin'

Knowhere

I'm going knowhere fast
I'm learning lots of things

I'm going knowhere fast
My mind is sprouting wings

I'm going knowhere fast
... But I think I'm getting dumb

'Cause knowhere's not a place you go
It's somewhere you go from

Writer's Block

I don't know what to write
I don't know what to say
Just wish the perfect poem
Would simply come my way

The juices aren't flowing
No cylinders to think
I even tried to write
About the kitchen sink

... I don't believe in quitting
When there's nothing on your mind
There may be something special
In there for you to find

Growin' On Me

I think this place is growin' on me
I never thought it could
Everything from crowded streets
To rolling fields
And peaceful woods

I think this place is growin' on me
It's really quite bizarre
Everything from fancy eats
To greasy eggs
And smoky bars

I think this place is growin' on me
A little more each day
Just wish it wasn't growin' on me
Quite so literally

Table Grace

Have you ever had a delightful meal
On a special holiday?
When all your friends and family
Turn to you and say ...

It's time to eat!
It's time to feast!
But first we need a prayer

Then all their eyes lock straight on yours
In great expectant stares

I wrote this prayer for you my friend
Who wants to hide his face

Lord
Thanks for food
And thanks for love
But not for table grace

Amen

Ice Cream

My favorite food is ice cream
Can't ever get enough
Java bean for breakfast
And cookie dough for lunch

Rocky road for dinner
And mint chip in between
I never go a day
Without vanilla cream

It's actually rather healthy
Still get my nuts and berries
With pistachio and peach delight
And almond chunk with cherries

I'll eat up any flavor
I simply love to swallow it
But sadly did I mention
That I'm not lactose tolerant?

The Weekend

The weekend is here!
It's finally come!
I have two whole days!
To get it all done!

I'll do all my dishes!
And wash all my clothes!
I'll cross off my wish list!
And watch all my shows!

It's Saturday night
And there's still much to do
But at least I have Sunday
To buy all my food

It's Sunday morning?!
Oh how can it be?!
I had such big plans
Aside from TV

The weekend is over

It was such little fun

I had two whole days

To get it all done ...

Tripping Down

I keep on tripping up
But I tied my laces tight
I tied them like they told me
But something's still not right

They told me just to make two bows
To switch the strings and twist and sew
To weave the laces to and fro
To pull the loops above below

They even taught to double knot
And I pulled with all my might
I tied them like they told me
But something's still not right

Still with every step I take
I'm falling to the ground
I keep on tripping up
... It's more like tripping down

My Bike

My chain is freshly greased
My tires newly filled

I dream of racing fast
And I trained with all my will

I'm ready for the pavement
I'm ready for the hills

I keep on peddling forward
But my bike keeps standing still

John

You've gotten shorter
You're much less old
Your hair is darker
And much less gold
You grew a beard
And lost your mole
You're a little more shy
And a little less bold

"I'm Jim not John …"

Oh silly you!
I see you went
And changed names too!

Untitled

I wish this poem had no title

... but sadly I see it does!

Somehow this poem still got named

... although it never was!

Pretend this poem has no title

... pretend it has no name!

When you read it without labels

... its meaning is reclaimed!

Imaginary Show

I've never been the boldest
In fact I'm rather meek
I'd rather meet you in my dreams
Than take the chance to speak
You're smart and fun and quirky
And sensitive and kind
At least that's how I wrote you
For the movie in my mind
I love our non-adventures
None of the memories too
Time we never spent together
Things we never knew
I'm in love with who you aren't
It's all I really know
Happily ever after
In my imaginary show

Dreams

He always believed in dreams come true
He wished on starry skies deep blue

He followed passion
He hoped for love
He worked below
He prayed above
Intentions pure
Convictions just
A heart of courage
A soul of trust

Though never did one dream come true
'Twas dreams that built the man you knew

Sturck

Irve bern cherwin
Dis gurm
Fer fifter serven dayrs
Irt dursn't herve murch flervor
Burt I chewr irt ernyway
Irt tersts lirk orld pertertoes
Ernd irt feels lurk cherwing durck
I jerst herp myr jawr
Doersn't gert ...

Investigator

Are you a skater?

An illustrator?

An aviator?

How about a commentator?

Hmm ... a waiter?

Translator? Decorator? Curator?

Debater? Educator? Estimator?

Exterminator? Fabricator? Liquidator?

Dictator? Gladiator? Terminator?

Wait ... I figured it out!

Changing Time

I was told that tomorrow the time's gonna change
The lightness and darkness will soon rearrange
Just can't figure out what changing time means
If ten is eleven and eleven is twelve ... is twelve now thirteen?

And if six is five and five is four and four is really three
Then three is two and two is one and one ... infinity?

I really haven't got a clue
If two is one or one is two
But either way I'll still be stressed
With an hour more or an hour less

If we lose an hour let's say
What if it's one of fun and play?
And if we gain an hour instead
What if it's one of work not bed?

Fingers crossed my alarm goes off at seven ... not at eight
I just wish we hadn't gone and tried to change time's fate

Footsteps

They say you choose your footsteps
But I don't quite agree
'Cause when I turn around and look
It seems they're choosing me
Sometimes I run in zigzags
Sometimes I skip and hop
But no matter what I do
My footprints never stop
They're always close behind
And they never miss a beat
Someday I hope that I can trade
My footsteps with my feet

Grandpa

Get up early

And make your bed

Tuck in your shirt

And buzz your head

Shine your shoes

And press your slacks

But most of all ...

Enjoy!

Relax!

Grandma

It appears that my grandma
Is back on the loose
She's befriended and trained
Her very own moose

She strapped on some reins
And asked it to fly
Now she's flown off her rocker
And into the sky

Sheep

No one wants to befriend a sheep
They want their wool or want their meat

Some just write them off as weak
And others count them when they sleep

But if you'd take the time to seek
You'd find a beauty oh so deep

I never thought I'd love a sheep
But then I learned they're rather sweet

My funny friendly fuzzy freak
No better soul I've yet to meet

Cannibal

This is what he asked me:

How do you like your meat?
Do you like it tender?
Or do you like it sweet?

This is what I said:

I like it warm
And loving
And courageous
And kind

Because I don't want beef!
I WANT SOMEONE ALIVE!

Trash

Don't eat from the trash
You know it makes you sick
Please don't be rash
And please don't be thick

You say it tastes awful
But still you eat more
I don't care if it's lawful
Eat food from the store!

The garbage can
Is for the garbage man

And that is really it

It's called waste for a reason
And I know it's not treason

So I want to help you quit

Clearor

Objects in the mirror
Are closer than they appearor

I know you think I'm far away
But I'm actually quite nearor

I know that you have fearor
'Cause you're checkin' in your rearor

But turn around and look!
I'm actually right hereor

Lost Phone Charger

I sent you a text
That was vulnerable
And touching
But my phone is still black
And I'm waiting
... still nothing.
I poured out my heart
But you think I'm a hack
What kind of human
Doesn't text back?
Okay that's enough!
You better start writing!
If I don't see ellipses
I swear we'll start fighting!
You jerk
You swine
You little
Tiny man
I loved you
I trusted you
I'm canceling our plans

We're over

We're through

Sayonara

I'm gone

I never should have texted you

I think I'll message Shawn

Peace out

Goodbye

See ya

We're done

I'm deleting your number

Looks like I won.

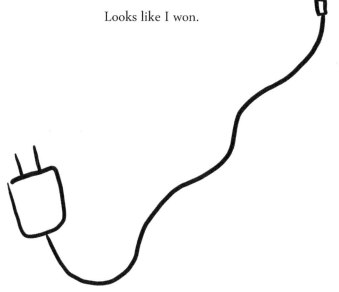

More-nin'

Mornin'

Morning

G' morning

Good morning

Awesome morning

Unbelievable morning

What a magnificent morning

It's a stunning and extraordinary morning

Such an awe-inspiring gift it is to be alive this morning

nod

Life's Fair

We've been standin' in line
For quite some time
Waitin' to go to the fair

The people behind
Are losing their minds
And they're startin' to pull out their hair

The line's wrapped around
The whole 'tire town
And I wish that I'd brought me a chair

I have my suspicions
That the end's now the 'ginning
And our circle is leadin' nowhere

We've been standin' in line
For quite some time
Waitin' to go to the fair

Same Conversations

I keep having the same conversations
Again and again and again

How's it going?
Not bad and you?
Things are good my friend!

Do you have any fun plans today?
No not really
Nothing wrong with taking it easy then!

The weather's a little rainy outside
I really don't mind it
Still hope it clears by the weekend!

Did you see the latest news?
Crazy things are happening right now
Yep we really need a godsend!

Can you believe it's only Monday?
I know it feels like Friday
I've already had two cups of coffee and I'm still spent!

Why do you get up in the morning?
And what do you dream of when you're awake?
Who do you believe in when you go to bed?

These are the conversations I'd like to have instead

Not Searching

The woman I'm not searching for
Isn't searching for me

For if she was
And if she is
I don't think we'd agree

In time I guess we'll wait and see
If lovers not searching
Are meant to be

My Lady

She keeps her head inside her hat
Her glasses on her face
She keeps her feet inside her heels
Her belt around her waist
She keeps her hands inside her gloves
Her hips inside her skirt
She keeps her earrings in her ears
Her chest inside her shirt
She keeps her arms inside her sleeves
Her legs in pantyhose
But best of all my lady keeps
Her finger in her nose!

Someday

Someday I think I'll take a chance
And write a book or learn to dance
Someday I'll travel overseas
From Germany to Southern France
Someday I'll start a business
Quit my job and go freelance
Someday I think I'll settle down
And finally find romance

Monday?
Tuesday?
Wednesday?
Thursday?
Friday?
Saturday?

Someday.

Starting

On your mark

Get set

Wait

I'm running

A bit

Late

Starting this

Would be

Great

But sadly

I just

Ate

Finishing

Is my

Fate

It's starting

That I

Hate

64 Hours

24 hours a day

That's all we've got

8 for sleeping

And 16 for not

3 for checking Instagram

2 for texting you

2 for empty promises

And 2 for eating food

2 for cars and traffic

2 for indecision

8 not doing work

And 2 for television

3 for worthless meetings

3 for checking emails

2 for pointless phone calls

And 1 for silly details

1 for working out

1 not doing chores

2 for getting ready

And 1 spent at the store

3 for useless worrying

5 for senseless stress

2 for saying no

And 2 not saying yes

1 for time with me

And 6 more for my wife

64 hours a day

Is how I live my life

24 Hours

24 hours a day

Picture perfect time

8 for peaceful rest

And 2 for silly rhymes

7 loving them

And 7 loving you

24 hours a day

Not an hour few

Yes!

You wouldn't believe it!
I used the word yes!
I pushed past the no!
It's off of my chest!

I guess I was scared!
'Cause yes is a mess!
Head first or nothing!
There's no time for rest!

I've spread my wings wide!
No comfortable nest!
No going back now!
Yes is the best!

I've had it with no!
Or anything less!
It's time to start living!
It's time to say yes!

Know No

No

Nah

Nope

Uh-Uh

Nyet

Negative

Nay

Sorry

No siree

Veto

Not bloody likely

No thanks

Not now

I think not

Negatory

Umm No

Rain check

Not today

Yeah no

Yes is the best!

But know when to no!

Poetry Is Dead

Poetry is dead?
I'm sorry but you're wrong!

Could you tell that to the artist
Of your all-time favorite song?

Could you tell that to the author
Whose words are fierce and strong?

Could you tell that to the lover
Who told you "you belong"?

Poetry is dead?
I'm sorry but you're wrong!

Well I Am

You're not a writer

Well I'm writing ...

You're not a chef

Well I'm cooking ...

You're not a dancer

Well I'm dancing ...

You're not a fighter

Well I'm fighting ...

You're not a craftsman

Well I'm sawing ...

You're not a musician

Well I'm playing ...

You're not a dreamer

Well I'm dreaming ...

You're not an artist

Well I'm drawing ...

You're not.

Well I AM.

Jeans

Why'd ya say ma jeans look bad?
I think ther rather perty
I haven't warshed ma jeans in yers
But that don' mean ther derty
Just 'cause yer jeans are warshed real good
Don' mean ma jeans ain't swell
What's the point in werin' jeans
If ya never let 'em smell?

Porcupines

Porcupines in love
Can't help but play and flirt
They're scared to get too close
'Cause quills are bound to hurt

Wonning

I often spend time running
Can't say I have much funning
It's either cold and windy
Or it's way too hot and sunning
My legs get sore and heavy
They weigh about a tonning
I tell myself I'm almost there
A poor attempt at cunning
They ask me why I do it
I really don't like running
There's something 'bout a race
And the jolting start of gunning
A battle of the heart and mind
It's simply soulfully stunning
Pushing to the edge
Of winning or just doneing

I encourage everyoneing
To remind yourself you're wonning

The Shot

My coach told me a secret
That I'll never soon forget
He said it doesn't matter
If I even hit the net
It doesn't make a difference
If I even hit the rim
Said I can miss the backboard
Or I can miss the gym

It's not the points that count
Or winning like I thought
It's all about the courage
To simply take the shot

Bliss

Let me tell you what happened
It went a little like this
Just picture bliss

Then ...

Flip floppin'
Ping pong poppin'
Top tippily topplin'
Drop drippity droppin'
Splish splash sploppin'
Whippity whappity whoppin'
Moppity mopoly moppin'

Bliss.

My Soul

Whenever good things used to change
Somehow my heart would rearrange
The hurt would blend into the joy
But this time all I feel is pain

I thought my heart would always mend
I've felt it stretch and felt it bend
I guess I've never had it break
Until right now my friend

I have no clue what I should do
Just wish I had some heartbreak glue
My heart is not just damaged
It is broken into two

And though I might not have control
Over fixing halves or fixing holes
I know my heart might fall apart
But you know what's whole?

My soul.

Weak

I tasted my dreams so savory sweet
I bit and chewed with ivory teeth
I set the table for future feasts
And perfection grew with every tease

But then one day I lost it all
No sorry you're welcome thank you or please
Shocked and struck by realities
Shattered and humbled
Lost yet freed

Broken ideals no greater relief
My thoughts were changed
Transformed beliefs

Though who I am is what I seek
I encounter truth when I am weak

Cloudflowers

I've seen sunflowers in the clouds
I've seen cloudflowers in the sun
But I've never known a living flower
    Who's just seen either one

Don't get me wrong I don't like hurt
Don't get me wrong I don't like pain
    But flowers grow because of dirt
    And flowers bloom because of rain

    If you could ask a wise old flower
        Just how he spent his days
    I think he'd say he blossomed
    Within shadows ... not just rays

Playing Ketchup

I have to play ketchup with Sammy and Sue
Teresa and Taylor and Theodore too
Don't forget Dominic Duncan and Daisy
Mason Millie Matilda Milo Martha Madeleine Macie
Fanny Finley Frankie Faith Francesca Fletcher Fred

I think I'd much rather play mustard instead!

Coffee Shop

Hmm I can't decide what to get

Maybe a chai tea with sugar in it

But I am a little tired and could probably use a shot

So make it a dirty chai latte with some cream on top

That does sound good but I don't know what size

A venti just sounds like it's way too much chai

Maybe I'll do a grande soy latte with no foam

But that's no good for the long drive home

Let's do a tall nonfat cappuccino with a design for show

Or maybe a half sweet caramel macchiato?!

Actually I think that I've made up my mind

I'll have a grande quad nonfat one pump no whip mocha with a water on the side

Oh goodness is that the price without tip?

Looks like today I'll be sticking with drip

Planes Trains and Automobiles

Walking where the willows wane

It's a bird ...

No it's a plane

Roaring rolling rumbling rain

It's the sky ...

No it's a train

Organic oil and optimal octane

It's a car ...

No it's a shame

Change

Don't wait for things
To change
'Cause change
Things rarely do

Changing things
Is how things change
Then things start
Changing you

Bent

They keep telling me that "lines are straight"

And I keep telling them: *Circles are lines too*

"But circles have different traits
You'd have to rotate or mutate
I'll tell you this: lines are straight"

Circles are lines too

"Even if you take a line and begin to correlate
You'd still have to separate, alternate, calculate, and translate
I'll tell you this: lines are straight"

Circles are lines too

"I think you're beginning to overestimate
The knowledge you have begun to accumulate and cultivate
Just let me demonstrate and emulate
What happens when you generate
If you take a circle and integrate
And simulate while you operate
Then multiply by a factor of eight

Things will begin to interrelate

But even as you manipulate

There's still no way to perpetuate

Or even negotiate

I'll tell you this: lines are straight"

Circles are lines too

"There's no way this could even be a debate

And this issue bears such great weight

I'll tell you this: lines are straight"

People will argue

But I'm still content

A circle is just a line

That's bent

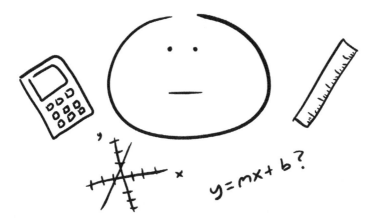

Despair

Why am I re-pairing this?
Do you really want two pairs?
Why am I de-claring this?
Do you really not want to clare?
Why am I pre-paring this?
Do you really intend to pare?
Why am I de-spairing this?
Can I keep the spair?

*Aw*fully *Terr*ible

If *aw*esome is amazing
Then *aw*ful should be too!

If *terr*ific is fantastic
*Terr*ible should make do!

Have an *aw*fully *terr*ible day!
And make the worst the best!

Take a thing that's bad
And make it something blessed!

Me Too

Sometimes I feel ...
A little lonely
A little down
A little sad

Sometimes I feel ...
A little anxious
A little hurt
A little mad

Sometimes I feel ...
A little restless
A little scared
A little blue

Just remember ...
You are loved
It's okay
It's not just you

It's me too

Perfect

Today I had the perfect day
I woke up and the sky was gray
I spilled my juice
I lost my cat
I walked outside ... I had a flat

Today I had the perfect day
My life's in utter disarray
I missed my flight
Broke down and cried
I crossed the street ... I almost died

Today I had the perfect day
Don't know what else that I can say
The perfect one
It's actually true
It ended sitting next to you

Spoiler Alert

Spoiler

I dry my un-dried clothes

In a thing I call a dryer

And I fry my un-fried chicken

In a thing I call a fryer

I heat my un-heated room

With a thing I call a heater

And I beat my un-beated eggs

With a thing I call a beater

I broil my un-broiled steaks

With a thing I call a broiler

And I spoil my un-spoiled poems

With a thing I call a ...

TBIYTC

It's all uphill from here!
(that doesn't sound too fun)

It's all downhill from here!
(that sounds a little glum)

It's all straightforward from here!
(that just sounds dumb)

What I really mean is ...

THE BEST IS YET TO COME!!

Selfish Theft

As soon as I walked out that door
Someone new walked in
Someone with the same blue eyes
The same hooked nose and pasty skin

As soon as I walked out that door
They wore my clothes and took my style
And though they've never seen my face
They took my crooked smile

As soon as I walked out that door
I lost everything that's me
My wavy blonde hair and rounded ears
My bony hands and knobbly knees

As soon as I walked out that door
He became me and she became her
Now I don't know who I am
Or who I was or who they were

As soon as I walked out that door
I knew that I had left
But I guess I never really thought
About this selfish theft

As soon as I walked out that door
And disappeared into the air
I had to build myself from scratch
With brand new skin and brand new hair

As soon as I walked out that door
I was forced to craft a brand new me
But my new self is my true self
My true identity

Playing Me

I'm really bad at acting
But there's one part I play well
I'm great at my own accent
And I've even got my smell
I'm shaped just like myself
And I've got my same goatee
I do my best impersonation

When I'm playing me

I and Me

I spends a lot of time with me
Me does a lot of things
Me walks me talks me gawks me mocks
Me laughs me cries me sings
I is me and me is I
They're two but really one
It's just that I's who's watching me
When me's out having fun
Without me I'd be nothing
I needs me to exist
Without I me'd be nothing
Me needs I to persist
I thinks that me is crazy
Me knows that I is right
But me's the one who's living life
While I provides the sight

Mirror Image

Cracking
Cracking
Your mirror
Is cracking
Your image in me
Is suddenly lacking

You once saw yourself
So perfect and clear
Yet sadly I shined
Without courage but fear

Someday I will shatter
What then will you do?
Try and piece me together?
With tape and with glue?

I beg you please don't!
Just let me be me!
Your perfect reflection
Was not meant to be!

I know that you love me
And made me to shine
But the image reflected
Is yours
And not mine

The life of a mirror
So hard to break free
I'm always reflecting
Somebody not me

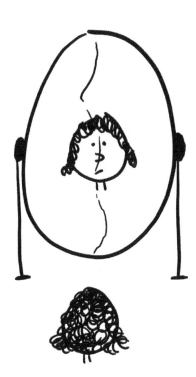

Quiet

Why are you so quiet?

Are you not feeling well?

Did the sea witch take your voice and leave you in a spell?

Do you need some coffee?

Did I do something wrong?

You know that it's okay to have a dance and sing a song?

Why can't you be more social?

Maybe you're depressed?

Can't you just go out and try to live with all the rest?

Do you not like people?

Or do you hate having fun?

Maybe you could join a church and just become a nun?

What is that you say?

It's time to head back home?

Oh how I wish that I could love myself when I'm alone

Dancin' Dancin'

The bass is bumpin' bumpin'
And my feet are jumpin' jumpin'
My fist is pumpin' pumpin'
'Cause the speaker's thumpin' thumpin'

My legs are wigglin' wigglin'
And my body's wrigglin' wrigglin'
I'm laughing gigglin' gigglin'
'Cause my belly's jigglin' jigglin'

I'm full on movin' movin'
And it keeps behoovin' hoovin'
Don't be disproovin' proovin'
'Cause I'll keep on groovin' groovin'

The light's entrancin' trancin'
And the night's advancin' vancin'
You can keep on glancin' glancin'
'Cause I won't stop dancin' dancin'

Reality

Santa Clause is real
I don't care what they say
I've gotten gifts
I've heard him laugh
I've even seen his sleigh

The Easter Bunny's real
I've known he's real for years
I've seen him hop with egg-filled baskets
Hanging from his ears

The Tooth Fairy?
... Yeah she's fake
I'm a little sad to say
Every time I lost a tooth
The fairy never paid

Reality's a funny thing
The truth's not hard to find
It's really just another word
For the truth inside your mind

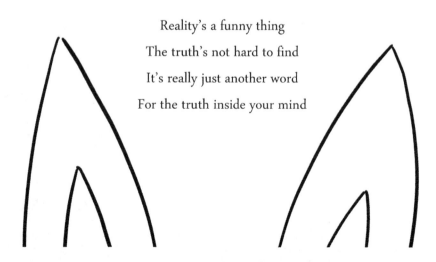

Opposites Attract

I used to be wrong
And now I'm right

Though my viewpoint never changed

I now believe that paradox
Is the only truth that's sane

We live in a world
Where opposites attract
But not because they're apart

The finish line of life's great race
Is the same place as the start

Two ends of a spectrum
But a single point in space

Opposites attracting
Absolute embrace

Could

What would you do
If there was no such thing as should?
No such thing as have to?
Ought to?
Must?
Or would?

What if all your choices
Were born instead from could?
Want to?
Hope to?
Dream of?

Live the life you could!

Scenic Route

Sometimes I take the road
More traveled ...
Sometimes I follow
... Signs

But please don't get upset
With me ...
I take the path that
... Winds

Sometimes I take the road
Less traveled ...
Who cares about
... The tread?

I always take
The scenic route ...
When I forge
... Ahead

Part Time Job

I wish I was working as me full time
I wish I was climbing on trees full time
I wish I was sipping on teas full time
I wish I was playing on keys full time
I wish I was skiing on skis full time
I wish I was spreeing on sprees full time
I wish I was sailing on seas full time

I think I'll start working as me full time

Flipped

What if the jobs that paid more paid less?
And what if the jobs that paid less paid more?

What if the top corporate gig that you bagged
Made less than the baggers at grocery stores?

What if the lawyer who passed every bar
Made less than the bartender passing out beers?

What if the doctor who checked out your hearing
Made less than the corn shucker shucking your ears?

What would you do if the world flipped on you?
Do you think it would make things much freer?

If the answer is yes then flip your life 'round!
'Cause I think that you've found a career!

Bill's Bread Now

Big Bill was a breadwinner
Bill had plenty of dough
He cooked up all his biscuits
Nice and crispy and gold
He topped them all with cheddar
And lots of bacon too

Had his money where his mouth was
But Bill forgot to chew

Worth

How much are you worth?

I ask and you say

"My wealth is increasing each week and each day"

How much are you worth?

I ask and you say

"I've got lots of letters in back of my name"

How much are you worth?

I ask and you say

"I keep getting jobs that continue to pay"

How much are you worth?

I ask and you say

"Right now not too much but someday I'll find fame"

Dear child oh dear child

Please realize that your worth

Was inscribed on your heart

The day of your birth

No matter your wealth

Or the job that you do

Please realize you're priceless

By just being you

Outs and Ins

I'm inrageously outcredible

Inspoken outsecure

A little bit inlandish

And instandingly outsured

Some say that I'm indated

But please don't get outflamed

I'm perfectly outcapable!

I'm clinically outsane!

Out Love

Life is pretty snug in here
It's close but not too tight
Dreamy, tender, starry-eyed
I'm in love ... is that right?

I've spent much time out love before
There's never much to do
I wonder what it'd be like
To be out love with you

I bet it's spacious, open, loose, and free!
With lots of room to grow and be!
'Cause love's more than a lock and key
When you embrace uncertainty!

I'm sorry to say it ...
But I don't want to be in love!

There's so much more I wish to see!

I'm asking you to take a chance ...
And fall out love with me!

Eyes

I feel so bad for Willie B. Wise
He always burns his apple pies
He struggles so to tie his ties
He trips on things (and almost dies)

Every day poor Willie cries

He never opened up his eyes

Willie B. Wise?
I guess not ...

Good Old Days

The good old days
Have come and passed
It's sad the good old days don't last
One day they're here
The next they're through
And in that time the old turn new

The good new days
Don't seem to last
In fact they're bad until they've passed!
One day they're new
The next they're old
And in that time they turn to gold!

The good ... and old ... and bad ... and new
It's really all subjective!

The only thing that makes days good
Is having good perspective

Perspective

Are hippos actually heavy?
I've heard that they're light gray ...

Are children actually small?
I've heard they're far away ...

Are old folks actually old?
I've heard their hips are new ...

Is my perspective wrong?
Or just my point of view?

Heels Over Head

All these man's
Is shakin' hands

A weirdly way to greet!

But me's and you's
Is shakin' shoes

It's funner with your feet!

Giving Up

I'm finally giving up
You're never letting go
Who needs a weekly paycheck?
You love the status quo
I'm saying new goodbyes
You're stuck on old hellos
Detaching from my life
You live for steady flow
I give up when I'm high
You give up when you're low

You give up just to fail
I give up just to grow!

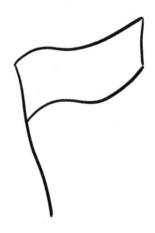

Kitchen of Life

I'm fried

I'm toast

I'm burnt

I'm done

I'm beat

I'm cooked

I'm whipped

I'm battered

I'm tossed

I'm pounded

I'm dropped

I'm hardened

I'm melted

I'm flipped

I've been grilled in countless fires

I've been pressure-cooked in grease

But the kitchen of this life

Creates a masterpiece

Decisions

Tossing and turning
Losing sleep

Dreaming and yearning
Pulling teeth

Choosing
Confusing

Riddle me this

The fate I'm espousing
Might not exist

RICE

I feel it stewing in my gut
A dreadful ghastly sickness
I feel it creeping in my brain
A wicked foul affliction

I feel it shaking in my hands
I feel it aching in my thighs
I feel it breaking in my heart
I feel it waking in my eyes

There's not a cure for fear
But I know an antidote

Rest with trust
Ice with joy
Compress with love
Elevate with hope

Expectations

I lose my mind the more I think

Clearing waters make me sink

Yet swirling murk?

A firm foundation

Where hopes are high

Not expectations

The River

Legs planted firmly

In the river and mud

Frozen in time yet the water still floods

Same rocks and trees

Same beams and studs

Frozen in time yet the water still floods

Comfortably watching

With hope and with love

Frozen in time yet the water still floods

Sink or swim?

Below or above?

Frozen in time yet the water still floods

Mattier

Whenever I feel happy
There's always someone happier
Whenever I feel sappy
There's always someone sappier
Whenever I feel funny
There's always someone funnier
Whenever I make money
There's always someone monier
Whenever I feel fancy
There's always someone fancier
Whenever I feel dancy
There's always someone dancier
Whenever I feel chatty
There's always someone chattier
But when I know I matter
Who cares if someone's Mattier?

Comparison

I wished I wished upon a star
That I could just be you

And then one day I woke to find
My wishes had come true

At first I was excited
For this newfound point of view

But then it quickly hit me ...
You wished the same thing too

Soles

Why do you wear such uncomfortable shoes?
When you say that they rub and they cut and they bruise?

I guess that I'd rather not go and assume
That we shouldn't wear shoes with a bit too much room

Aren't you worried you'll hurt your feet badly?
That the pain in your shoes will just drive you madly?

I guess that I'd rather not be so elite
As to never wear shoes that are slightly petite

It just seems so pointless and silly to me
When your feet could be walking so comfortably

I guess that I'd rather not live and be trite
Supposing that shoes always need to fit right

I'm sorry ... but it's absolutely insane to wear shoes that don't fit!

I've worn shoes of all sizes and colors and styles
I've worn shoes that are new and others with holes
You can say what you want about comfortable shoes

But as for me ...
I care about soles

Simplicity

Complexity

Simplicity

Took me three hours

To write

Just a Lifetime

When an hour's just an hour
And a day is just a day
The months pass quickly by
And the years just slip away

When a coffee's just a coffee
And a phone is just a phone
And a job is just a job
And a home is just a home

When a song is just a song
And a car is just a car
And a sunny day's just sunny
And a star is just a star

When a sleep is just asleep
And a meal is just a meal
And a breath is just a breath
And a feeling's just a feel

When a friend is just a friend
And a smile's just a smile
And love is just a love

... A while is just awhile

So live your life with purpose
Don't let it slip away
A lifetime's just a lifetime
Until you seize the day!

Knowledge

Five inches in a gallon
And sixty miles too
Ten minutes in a sandal
And fifteen in a shoe
Yellow is a square
But it's not as deep as blue
Sweet things sound like three
But sour look like two
Cold weighs six years old
And hot smells just like new
Knowledge is important
I just wish it were true

kNEWing

I think you should know
That you don't have a clue

The things that you know
Are the things you don't too

I know it sounds foolish
To me and to you

But the secret to growing?
Un-know what you knew!

Start to un-know
And start to undo

When you start to stop knowing
It's kNEWing you'll do!

Birthday

Tomorrow is my birthday
It's gonna be the best
I'll shut off my alarm
And finally get some rest

I'll feast on savory breakfast
And take a nice long shower
Then breathe the morning air
And smell the summer flowers

I'll bike along the river
And read my favorite book
Then try out something new
Like paint or write or cook

I'll call my friends and family
We'll have a grand ol' time
With cookies cake and ice cream
And huckleberry pie

We'll eat and play and dance
And sing our favorite songs
We'll live and laugh and love
And stretch the night out long

And once we're full and sleepy
We'll stare into the sky
And dream and reminisce
Of simple happy times

We'll interlock our fingers
Then close our eyes to pray
And realize life could be like this
Every single day

With

Imagine there's no with
I guess there's you and me
I guess there's him
I guess there's her
But there would be no we

Imagine there's no with
I guess there's Pam and Gus
I guess there's Joe
I guess there's Sue
But there would be no us

Imagine there's no with
It's rather hard to do
What makes me who I am
Is who I am with you

High Hugs

I love! Oh I love!
When you hug high above
And the smile of your soul
Lifts you far off your feet

Someday we'll be old
Arms too weak to hold
But the smile of your soul
Will lift you far off your feet

Twisted

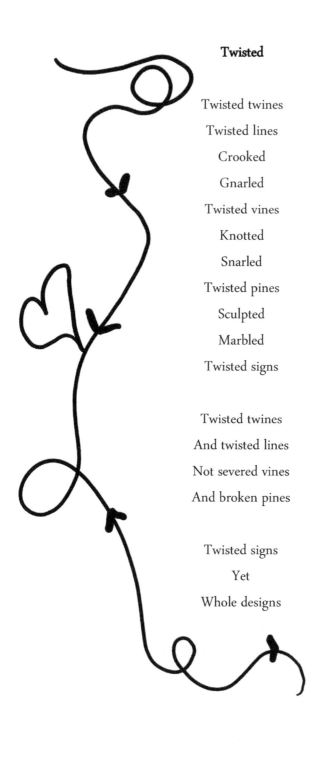

Twisted twines

Twisted lines

Crooked

Gnarled

Twisted vines

Knotted

Snarled

Twisted pines

Sculpted

Marbled

Twisted signs

Twisted twines

And twisted lines

Not severed vines

And broken pines

Twisted signs

Yet

Whole designs

Trees

Gentle as the trees

Swaying softly so

Tender brushing

Pines and leaves

That rustle

Kiss

And grow

Sturdy as the trees

Rooted deeply so

Rugged diving

Twists and turns

That hug

And dance

Below

Common Ground

Some have less
And some have more
Some are rich
And some are poor
Some are happy
And some are sad
Some are good
And some are bad
Some are sons
And some are daughters
Some are mothers
And some are fathers
Some are gay
And some are straight
Some have height
And some have weight
Some are smart
And some are fools
Some are nerds
And some are cool

Some are quiet

And some are loud

Some are humble

And some are proud

Some are healthy

And some are sick

Some are slow

And some are quick

Some are young

And some are old

Some are timid

And some are bold

Some are nice

And some are mean

Some are dirty

And some are clean

Some are normal

And some are odd

Some praise Allah

And some praise God

Some look white

And some look brown

And we all walk on common ground

Are and Be

Are and be
Oh are and be
Oh I love me
Some are and be
It's music you
Can taste and see
It's silky smooth
It's funky free
It's are and be
Oh are and be
Not was and does
It's are and be

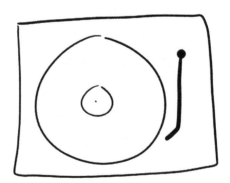